Composers in this book :

HANDEL (1685-1759)

HAYDN (1732-1809)

SCHUBERT (1797-1828)

An explanation of musical terms used in this book

Aria An air or song in an opera or oratorio.

Anthem A short choral work using religious words. An anthem might have an organ part or it could be unaccompanied.

Cantata A story or play set to music to be sung by a chorus, but not acted.

Chamber Music Music suited to a room or small hall, and played by three, four or more players.

Counterpoint The combining of two or more melodies to produce a musical result.

Divertimento A light and not too serious work, usually for small orchestra and containing several movements.

Folk-song A song which has been passed on from one age to another. As the music was not written down, different versions of the same tune can often be found.

Harmony The sounding together of notes to produce the musical effect known as chords.

Kapellmeister Musical director in the service of a prince or nobleman.

Libretto The text of an opera or an oratorio.

Mass A musical setting of the principal Roman Catholic service.

Opera A play which is mostly sung, and which has costumes, scenery, acting and music to go with the singing.

Operetta Word used to define a 'light opera'.

Oratorio A composition, usually based on a religious theme, for solo voices, chorus and orchestra, dramatic in character but performed without action, costumes or scenery.

Overture A piece of music which precedes an opera or oratorio but which might well be played separately as a concert piece.

Quartet Music for four voices or instruments.

Quintet Music for five voices or instruments.

Serenade Music to be played or sung out of doors at night.

Symphony An elaborate composition for an orchestra, usually having three or four movements in different rhythms.

BOOK 2

Lives of the
GREAT
COMPOSERS

by IAN WOODWARD
with illustrations by MARTIN AITCHISON

Publishers: Wills & Hepworth Ltd., Loughborough

First published 1969   ©   *Printed in England*

Handel (1685-1759)

George Frederick Handel, composer of the famous oratorio *Messiah*, was born during the same year as Bach and died a few years after him. The two composers had other things in common: they both came from Germany, they were both supreme organists, both had an enormous influence on future musicians, and in old age they both suffered the distress of blindness.

In most other respects, such as their way of life and the sort of music they wrote, they were quite different. Handel, unlike Bach, was not fortunate enough to be born into a musical family. In fact Handel's father, who became one of the most prominent barber-surgeons in the town of Halle, did all he could to deter young George Frederick from taking music seriously.

George Frederick, in common with many born musicians, was a tough child and a natural fighter. When his father burnt his beloved toy instruments, he somehow managed to persuade his mother to smuggle a clavichord into the attic. Long after bedtime, the sound of the tinkling keyboard instrument could be heard in other parts of the house, and one night his angry father stormed into the attic and said firmly that George Frederick must forget once and for all any ideas he might have of becoming a professional musician.

4   *Handel's father storms into the attic.*

7214 0242 9

When Handel was seven, he went with his father on a trip to a town not very far from his native Halle, where the Duke of Saxony heard the young lad playing on the chapel organ. The Duke was so impressed that he persuaded Handel senior to allow George Frederick to receive lessons from the organist of the local chapel in Halle. Handel's father could not ignore so important a man and so the boy studied with the organist for three years, and during this period his fame on the keyboard spread throughout the land.

Just before his eleventh birthday, Handel was taken to Berlin where his organ playing caught the attention of the Electoral Court. "You must go to Italy to study, young man," said the Elector, but Handel's father, feeling he had little time left to live, no longer cared for Dukes or Electors and ordered George Frederick back home.

Arriving back in Halle, Handel found his father extremely ill. He died soon after. For a while Handel continued with his general education and studied law at university, though only out of a sense of duty to his late father. Music, though, was in his blood. So one summer's day in 1703, when he was eighteen, Handel packed his bags and set off from Halle to 'find music' in the big and exciting city of Hamburg.

The Duke of Saxony hears the young Handel playing on the chapel organ.

Handel arrived in Hamburg to find it a gay and prosperous city, with a fine opera house where he was offered a job as a harpsichordist and second violinist. The pay was poor, however, and the young musician found it necessary to do a little teaching when he was not employed at the opera house. Through the friendship of a fellow musician, Johann Mattheson, Handel soon became familiar with the musical circle of Hamburg and in it found many useful contacts.

Meanwhile his fame as a virtuoso on the organs of the city's churches made the boy the sensation of the moment. Not surprisingly, even though he was not particularly religious, his first important work was written for the Church. For a boy of nineteen, his *Passion of St. John* is an amazing achievement.

The following year, because the director of the opera house, Reinhard Keiser, was too busy with other things to embark on an opera, the job of writing *Almira* fell to Handel. This was Handel's first opera and displayed many ideas new to Hamburg. It was written very quickly and became an instant success.

Handel's continual good fortune made Mattheson and the theatre director very jealous, and there were frequent quarrels. One particular disagreement with Mattheson led to a duel, and only because Mattheson's sword broke on Handel's coat button was the composer's possible death averted.

8   *A coat button saves Handel's life.*

At this period, German opera was still greatly influenced by the Italian style, and every composer felt it his duty sooner or later to make a pilgrimage to the sunny land where composers like Cavalli and Scarlatti were raising considerably the standard of opera. Handel decided that he must go to the country whose music led the world.

In the great musical cities of Florence, Rome, Naples and Venice, Handel's music and harpsichord playing were an immediate success. His charm and wit endeared him to the households of the country's most influential families. In Florence his first Italian opera, *Rodrigo*, was performed under the patronage of the Grand Duke's son. In Rome, however, the Pope had ruled that no opera should be staged there. So Handel wrote for the Church, and works like his profound *Dixit Dominus* received much praise.

When he arrived in Venice, Handel won the friendship of two people who were to be largely responsible for his eventual journey to England – Prince Ernest of Hanover, whose brother was to become King George of England, and the music-loving Duke of Manchester.

After a stay in Venice, Handel returned to Germany to take up the post of kapellmeister to the Elector of Hanover. There he taught the harpsichord to Caroline of Ansbach, who later became the wife of George II and Queen of England.

Handel at the time of his Italian tour, and a composite view of the sort of buildings and scenery he saw in Venice.

What a dismal place London must have seemed to Handel when he first arrived there in 1710. The streets he walked were thick with mud, and everywhere could be seen the refuse people threw out of their windows. Robberies were commonplace, and it was unwise to walk the streets at night for fear of being attacked.

Nevertheless, Handel arrived in England at just the right time. English opera was almost non-existent, and it was the work of the great Italian composers which was setting the fashion in operatic music. In a fortnight he had written *Rinaldo*, which was performed with great success at the Queen's Theatre, Haymarket.

Handel was welcomed into the homes of the aristocracy, and Queen Anne received him graciously, awarding him a yearly salary of two hundred pounds.

Public concerts were then uncommon in London, but an eccentric tradesman named Thomas Britton frequently invited cultured aristocrats and lovers of music, whether rich or poor, to listen to music in the loft of his Clerkenwell coal business. Many an evening Handel would race enthusiastically up the steep stairs to the loft to play a small organ or harpsichord, to the delight of his audience. Other evenings would find him at the magnificent musical entertainments held at Burlington House by the young Duke of Burlington.

Thomas Britton listens to the music of Handel and others in the loft of his Clerkenwell coal business.

By the time he was thirty, Handel was the most talked-about musician in the country, and was rich enough to be able to afford to buy his own house in London. Among the works he composed at this time were the oratorio *Esther* and the choral cantata *Acis and Galatea*, which were both the first of their type to be written in England.

Handel was officially still kapellmeister to the Elector of Hanover, but because of his increased success in England he continually postponed his return there. When Queen Anne died and Hanover's George became King of England, George showed his annoyance at Handel's prolonged absence by pretending he did not exist as his kapellmeister. But soon after, at about the time Handel wrote his *Water Music*, the King and Handel were friends again.

In 1720, with Handel as Director of Music, the 'Royal Academy of Music' (*not* the Academy known by the same name today), was formed to present Italian-style opera at the King's Theatre. Here he wrote such fine operas as *Tamerlano*, *Scipio*, and *Rodelinda*.

Handel engaged singers from Italy at enormous fees. One of these singers, Francesca Cuzzoni, a short, ungainly, temperamental woman who enthralled London with her singing, insisted on singing an aria *her* way. Only after Handel flew into a rage and threatened to throw her out of the window did Cuzzoni agree to sing the aria *Handel's* way!

Handel threatens to throw Francesca Cuzzoni out of the window.

Handel was by now an English subject, and Composer to the Court. For the coronation of George II he wrote four splendid Coronation Anthems, including *Zadok the Priest*, which has since been sung at every English coronation.

Success brought Handel many jealous enemies. As a man who came from Germany, he found himself in the middle of violent musical and political squabbles between the German George II and the English Prince of Wales. A rival opera company was formed to bring about Handel's ruin, but he won the Prince to his side when he wrote a wedding anthem and the opera *Atalanta*.

The intrigues, however, made Handel very ill. In June 1737 the doors of his opera house were closed. Handel was bankrupt. After recuperating at Aix-le-Chapelle, he returned to England to settle his debts and composed with his old energy. First came the comic opera *Serse* (from which comes the tune now known as 'Handel's Largo'), then two oratorios, *Saul* (with its solemn 'Dead March') and *Israel in Egypt* (which has a magnificent 'Hailstone Chorus').

For a while Handel hired a theatre in Lincoln's Inn Fields, where he staged his latest operas, *Imeneo* and *Deidamia*. Yet all this time he was still enduring attacks from his enemies, who made his theatre seasons chaotic by hiring men to tear down posters and create riots outside the theatre.

16   *Hired thugs try to reduce attendances at Handel's operas.*

Ruined in health and fortune, and terribly discouraged, Handel decided in 1741 to abandon opera. Instead he turned to religious music. He had already written *Saul* and *Israel in Egypt*, and several more oratorios followed, including *Judas Maccabaeus* (which is all about fighting), *Solomon*, *Samson* and *Joshua*. His most enduring oratorio, however, was to be *Messiah*, based on the Scriptures of the Bible and written in the incredibly short period of twenty-three days.

Handel hardly stirred from his room during those twenty-three days. His manservant would bring a meal, only to find the previous one untouched. When Handel had completed the second part, containing the 'Hallelujah Chorus', the servant found him with tears in his eyes, and the composer said, "I did think that I saw all Heaven before me, and the great God Himself."

When the King heard the majestic 'Hallelujah Chorus' he was so moved by it that he stood up out of respect, a tradition which audiences honour to this day.

For a fireworks display in Vauxhall Gardens, Handel wrote his *Fireworks Music*. The never-ending battle against his old enemies played havoc with his health, and his last years were made miserable with blindness. Handel died a week after collapsing during a performance of *Messiah*, which he was conducting, and he was buried with great ceremony in Westminster Abbey.

Handel writes his Messiah *oratorio.*

Haydn (1732-1809)

In the little Austrian village of Rohrau, not far from the Hungarian border and where Joseph Haydn was born in 1732, gay peasant dances and folk-songs could be seen and heard everywhere. The simple folk who tilled the land, or worked as millers, carpenters or weavers, had a great natural ability to 'make music'. No wonder Joseph became a musician with so much music around him.

Joseph was the second of twelve children born to a kindly couple of music-loving peasants. His father, Mathias Haydn, made and repaired wheels of all kinds. He was a master of his craft. In the evenings he would accompany his wife, Maria Anna, on the harp while she sang the same songs that the local folk sang in the village. Soon Joseph joined in.

One day when a strolling fiddler came to entertain the villagers, Joseph was so carried away that he picked up two sticks and followed the musician everywhere, imitating his playing. A schoolmaster relative of the Haydns, 'Cousin Franck', saw this charade and sensed early signs of a musical talent. Joseph's mother, however, had set her sights on her son entering the Church, but Franck managed to persuade her to allow the boy to be educated at his school in the nearby town of Hainburg.

Young Joseph Haydn imitates the playing of a strolling fiddler.

Franck, who was Joseph's first teacher at Hainburg, proved to be the composer's earliest and most lasting influence. Franck was a good teacher who stood no nonsense from his pupils, and Joseph had his fair share of beatings for disobedience. All the same, he was a good pupil, and by the time he was six he was singing masses in the church choir and making good progress with his violin and harpsichord studies.

When the drummer of the town's harvest celebrations fell sick, Franck had no alternative but to give the job to his six-year-old pupil. Joseph was so delighted that he immediately looked for and found an old flour bin, secured some cloth over its rim and with a couple of sticks marched proudly around the household. As he beat his 'drum' he sent up great clouds of dust, but his improvisation impressed everybody.

Shortly afterwards, the Imperial Court Composer, George Reutter, passed through Hainburg from Vienna in search of new choirboys. He asked Joseph to sing a trill. "But even Cousin Franck can't do *that*!" the eight-year-old boy exclaimed. After three attempts, however, Joseph succeeded in his trill. Reutter was more than pleased and said, "Bravo, Joseph! You shall come to Vienna with me."

Young Haydn plays his home-made drum.

Although for the first time in his life young Haydn was able to see in Vienna the sort of lives people led outside the comparatively backward town of Hainburg, Vienna offered few advantages to the boy other than the opportunity to meet influential people. When he was not engaged in his duties in the choir at St. Stephen's Cathedral, he was given an elementary education in Latin, religion, arithmetic and writing, and was able to continue learning the violin and harpsichord.

For most of the time Reutter was too busy with his duties as Court Kapellmeister to pay any attention to his choirboys, and his two assistants devoted more time to their own personal interests than to teaching their pupils. So Haydn realised he had to teach himself as much as possible if he was ever to write music. Quite often when the other boys were out playing, Haydn took his small harpsichord up into the attic and practised for hours at a time.

More and more, Haydn was longing to write music, but he received no encouragement whatsoever from Reutter. In fact, when Haydn one day attempted to compose a piece of twelve-part church music, Reutter merely laughed and said, "You silly lad, aren't two parts enough for you?" Haydn was not easily daunted, and by studying during what moments of free time he had, he gradually mastered the basic elements of composition.

Reutter discourages Haydn in his attempts at musical composition.

Haydn stayed at St. Stephen's until he was seventeen, when he was dismissed because his voice broke – and also because he cut off a fellow choirboy's pigtail! He was turned into the street without a penny in his pocket and with nowhere to go.

Quite soon he found lodgings with a member of the choir of another church, and for a while he earned his keep as a barber's boy. One of his jobs was the dressing of wigs. Gradually he managed to scrape together enough money to rent an old attic, where he took in a few pupils. With the money he earned, he bought a clavichord and six sonatas by Emmanuel Bach, using these as models for his early compositions. Soon after he was seventeen he wrote his first Mass.

Now, with several notable works behind him, including music for a farce which received a great deal of success throughout Vienna, Haydn's name was becoming more well-known. A rich nobleman, named Karl von Furnberg, heard of the young composer and engaged him as a violinist at his house at Weizirl. This was an important period for Haydn, because for the first time he was able to try out his own works on a full professional orchestra. At Weizirl he wrote his first quartet and first symphony, as well as several divertimenti and serenades.

Haydn works in a barber's shop.

In 1759 Haydn was appointed composer and director of music to Count Maximilian von Morzin, the Emperor's Chamberlain and Privy Councillor. The salary was meagre, but the post offered him board and lodgings and further opportunities to experiment with instrumental music.

During his two years' stay with the Count, he married one of the daughters of the barber for whom he once worked in Vienna. She was three years older than Haydn, who was then twenty-eight, and had a terrible temper. Maria, as she was called, found music – and the chores of looking after a home – quite intolerable, and they parted after a few years of unhappy marriage. Haydn never married again.

When the Count was compelled for economic reasons to cut down the number of people in his employment, Haydn was one of the unlucky ones who found himself out of a job. By a stroke of luck, however, Haydn had previously caught the attention of Prince Anton Esterhazy, one of Austria's richest nobles. As the Prince's kapellmeister was growing old, he engaged Haydn as an assistant at his estate at Eisenstadt, not far from Vienna. Haydn was very content – so content that he remained with the Esterhazys for the rest of his life.

Haydn's marriage proves a failure.

Haydn had been at Eisenstadt for only a year when Prince Anton died. The Prince's brother, Nicolaus, was even more fond of music, and when he succeeded Anton he built a fantastic fairy-tale palace which was modelled on Versailles. Prince Nicolaus called the palace Esterhaz. There were buildings of all kinds – an opera house, a puppet theatre, temples and summer-houses. The palace itself had one hundred and twenty-six magnificent rooms.

Life there was bliss for Haydn. He got on well with the Prince, was paid a comfortable yearly income of seven hundred and eighty-two florins, and was soon appointed kapellmeister. Haydn was expected to write music for every occasion, and produce something new and novel. It was not unusual for him even to produce plays.

The Prince so enjoyed life at Esterhaz that he was loathe to leave it or allow the musicians to see their families in Vienna. To remind the Prince that it was time they saw their families, Haydn composed his *Farewell Symphony*, in which, at the end, the players stop playing one by one and walk out with the music under their arms. The Prince took the hint and gave them a holiday!

Among the many other symphonies he wrote for the Prince, the *Toy Symphony* has become one of the most popular.

30

The Farewell Symphony *reminds the Prince that the musicians need a holiday!*

Even though Haydn hardly ever ventured far away from Esterhaz during the first half of his life, his fame nevertheless spread abroad. He was known in Russia, for whose Grand Duke he wrote his *Russian Quartets*, and publishers in London and Paris were clamouring for the honour to print his works. In 1785 he wrote *The Seven Words of our Saviour on the Cross*, which was commissioned by Cadiz Cathedral in Spain.

When Prince Nicolaus died in 1790, Haydn's name was already known throughout most of Europe. At last Haydn was free to see something of life away from Esterhaz, though the combined yearly pensions of one thousand four hundred florins from Haydn's two former employers stipulated that he should remain attached to the family as its kapellmeister.

Soon afterwards he was called to London by the impresario Salomon. He was offered high fees to write an opera, several symphonies and other works, and was welcomed at banquets, Royal courts and musical societies. He was always full of fun, as one of his symphonies shows. So that people would not fall asleep during the slow movement of this symphony, he interspersed it with sudden loud passages. He called it the *Surprise Symphony*, and a surprise it most certainly was for many people who were caught unawares during its first performance!

Haydn comes to London.

THE
LONDON
A
SYMPHONY
by
Joseph Haydn

With the money earned from further visits to England, Haydn was able to settle down to live peacefully for the rest of his life in a little cottage just outside Vienna. He had the *Oxford* and *Paris Symphonies* to his credit, as well as several fine string quartets and masses, and had taken as his pupil a young musician named Beethoven.

He had yet to tackle a full-scale oratorio, a state of affairs which was altered when Salomon suggested a libretto based on Milton's *Paradise Lost*. Out of this came first *The Creation* (which takes its place with Handel's *Messiah* and Mendelssohn's *Elijah*), followed by *The Seasons*. Performed in 1801, it proved to be Haydn's last major work.

His sight was now beginning to fail, and he spent the rest of his days composing charming little songs and inviting friends round to his cottage in the evenings to listen to the many stories he had to tell of his long life. He died a few days after the invading French armies fired a shot into his garden. Yet even the enemy honoured him, for just before he died a French officer sang Haydn an aria from *The Creation*, which deeply touched him. In his later years he was known affectionately as 'Papa' Haydn, for he was greatly loved by all who knew him.

A French officer honours the dying Haydn by singing an aria from The Creation.

Schubert (1797-1828)

Franz Schubert was one of those young men fortunate enough to be born into a family that regarded music very highly. Of all those composers (Gluck, Haydn, Mozart, Beethoven, Bruckner, Brahms) who made Vienna the world's music capital, he was the only true Viennese, having been born and bred there. Except for two brief visits into nearby Hungary, he spent the whole of his short life in the Austrian capital, and died there too.

Franz's father was a modest schoolmaster who, at twenty-two, married a cook named Elisabeth. As time went by they had fourteen children, although only five lived. Obviously there was never very much money to spare for luxuries, but the household was always a very happy one. The family's greatest pleasure was getting together to play their various musical instruments and to sing. Often the family formed a quartet to play for the rest of the family and friends who called round, with father playing the 'cello, Franz the piano or viola, and two brothers playing violins.

Although everyone in the Schubert household (except Elisabeth) played various musical instruments, Franz was the undoubted star, for he could play the violin, the piano and the viola by the time he was six. All the family sensed they had someone rather special among them, and father and older brother Ignaz taught him all they knew.

Members of the Schubert family enjoy a musical evening.

For a while Franz received further musical education from the organist of the local church, but the training was very limited and it was not until he was eleven that he received his most important tuition. His father, though not very well off, had nevertheless managed to scrape together just enough money to send him to Vienna's great choir school, which trained boys for the choir of the Imperial Court Chapel and provided a good general education at the same time. The boys of this school wore a striking uniform, very much like a soldier's.

There was music everywhere, and the atmosphere was just right for Franz. He joined the school orchestra and before long he became its first violinist. One of his responsibilities was to look after the instruments and, when necessary, to tune and re-string them. Quite often Franz took over the conductor's job on important occasions. When the orchestra practised in summer-time on the lush lawns of the school, people took such an interest in the music-making that chairs were provided for passers-by to watch the boys rehearsing.

All this time Franz was composing. He never stopped composing! Songs and piano pieces flowed from his pen as easily as words from the rest of us. However, one thing was missing, and that was a teacher who taught composition. He received the customary education in counterpoint and harmony, but not composition. At that time, what he knew about writing music was almost entirely what he had learned for himself.

The young Schubert tends the instruments of the school orchestra.

Soon, however, Franz was able to embark on a series of lessons in composition from Antonio Salieri, the great master of Italian opera. As composition was not part of the school curriculum, and recognising the boy's exceptional musical talent, the school authorities arranged for the boy to go into the town to visit Salieri for lessons. Franz was the only boy given the privilege of entering the town during term-time.

Salieri's influence resulted in Franz's first opera, *The Devil's Pleasance*, written when he was sixteen. His *First Symphony in D* was written the same year.

When the holidays came, Franz could hardly run home quickly enough to play in the family quartet, because music, as we have seen, was all that mattered to him. Later the family took on more players, and quite soon the Schuberts' tiny orchestra became well-known all over Vienna.

More than anything Franz loved to compose songs. In the thirty-one years of his life he wrote over six hundred of them. In fact he was to become known to future generations as the 'Father of the Lied'. *Lied* is the German word for 'song', and Schubert became the first composer to make a name for himself by the songs he set to the works of German poets. It is said that the '*lied*' really began with Schubert's first song, *Hagar's Lament*, and this song was most certainly a landmark in Schubert's career. It was composed in 1811, when he was just fourteen years old.

Schubert with the composer Salieri in a Vienna street.

At the age of seventeen, Schubert had to start thinking about earning a living. What he really wanted to do was to devote himself entirely to music, but that was as difficult to do then as it is now. For a while he took a job teaching young children music and ordinary subjects in his father's school, a job he disliked intensely, though the frequent holidays and short hours gave him plenty of time in which to compose. Two symphonies, six operas, numerous works for the Church and the piano, a quartet, and a hundred and fifty songs – this amazing amount of music was all produced by him in just one year – his eighteenth!

After two years of teaching at his father's school, he met a rich young man by the name of Franz von Schober who was convinced that Schubert was wasting his time and genius at the school. Indeed he was so convinced that he offered him free board and lodgings just so that the young Schubert could devote himself to writing music.

Schubert had already set songs to the verses of the great German poet, Goethe, including *Faust* and *The Erl-King*, but now he was entirely free from financial worries and poured out many more fine songs, piano sonatas and the *Fourth* and *Fifth Symphonies*. He was very fond of nature and in the afternoons, when he had finished composing, he loved to take long walks in the beautiful countryside of Vienna.

Franz Schubert teaches in his father's school.

Schubert had many friends in the world of art, poetry and music, and spent a great deal of his time with them, merrymaking, theatregoing, strolling on country outings, going to parties and meeting acquaintances at taverns and coffee houses. He enjoyed the company of other people, and he lived the sort of life that many young creative artists lived in places like Paris and Vienna during the last century. Always he was the life and soul of the party – so much so that a social evening with him became known as a 'Schubertiade': a 'Schubert Evening'. At one of these evenings he wrote one of his most beautiful songs, *Hark, Hark, the Lark!*, on the back of a bill.

Among the many contacts he made was a well-known singer of the Court Opera, named Vogl, who did much to make Schubert's name familiar in Vienna by singing his songs at parties and recitals. He even managed to get Schubert's operetta, *The Twin Brothers*, performed at the Imperial Theatre in the summer of 1820. *The Magic Harp*, another operetta, followed two months later. Now, despite the fact that he only once ever gave a concert of his own, Schubert was firmly established in the leading musical circles of Vienna.

In appearance Schubert was small and stocky; at twenty-one he was only five feet in height. His round wire spectacles were never off his face, and he even slept in them. Contrary to what we are usually led to believe, he hardly ever composed at the piano, but either sat or stood at a desk.

Schubert enjoys a stroll in the country with friends.

Although for some time Schubert's songs had become well-known in Vienna, through the concerts given by Vogl and other singers, hardly any of them had been printed. A group of friends decided they must do something about this and between them raised enough money to have twenty of Schubert's songs published. More and more people bought his songs, and Schubert had little difficulty in selling them. However, his chamber music and piano pieces were more difficult to sell, and he never saw any of his orchestral compositions in print during his lifetime.

One of these works – which never saw the light of day until seventy years after his death – is the *Symphony in B minor*, which is today known as *The Unfinished Symphony*. Schubert began work on this symphony in 1822, and intended to present it to the Musical Society, who had previously elected him an honorary member. Distractions with other work, however, prevented him from completing it – in fact, only the first two movements were ever written. No doubt he intended to finish it at some later date, but somehow never got around to it.

While composing the *Trout Quintet*, now one of his most popular pieces of chamber music, in the dead of night, the weary Schubert picked up the inkwell by mistake for the sandbox – used in those days instead of blotting paper. The 'blotchy' manuscript, and his letter describing it, can still be seen today.

The tired Schubert picks up the inkwell by mistake.

Schubert was often in love, though he never married. His first serious love affair was when he was seventeen, with a girl named Therese Grob, who sang the soprano solo of his *Mass in F*. "For three years I hoped to marry her," he wrote, "but could find no situation, which caused us great sorrow." Later, in 1824, when he went to teach the children for a brief spell at the home of the Esterhazys – where, you will remember, Haydn was once kapellmeister – he again fell in love, this time with one of the family's countesses, Caroline.

In fact, Schubert fell in and out of love as frequently as any healthy young man, but the old story that he poured out his romantic sufferings in his songs is not really true.

Schubert was a most prolific composer, and on occasions wrote as many as eight songs in a day. *The Fair Maid of the Mill*, a touching song-cycle, was composed in 1823, followed four years later by *The Winter Journey*. He also wrote fifteen string quartets, including the lovely *A-minor Quartet*.

Although he composed a number of operas, Schubert was never completely at ease in the theatre. He did, however, achieve some measure of success with his *Rosamunde*, which was first given at the Wien Theatre in 1823. All Vienna was soon humming melodies from the opera, though today only the beautiful overture is familiar to us.

Schubert falls in love with Caroline Esterhazy.

Schubert and Beethoven lived in the same city of Vienna for many years before they ever met. Beethoven was known throughout Europe, while Schubert was known only to a small, discerning audience in Vienna. Beethoven had not even heard of Schubert, though Schubert certainly knew and admired Beethoven.

Poor Schubert was so much in awe of the famous composer that, when a friend took him to see Beethoven, he was petrified and ran out of the room when the great man asked him a question.

Not long after writing his last great work, the profound *Ninth Symphony in C major* (known as *The Great*), Schubert ate some fish at one of the inns where he frequently dined. He pushed the food away, complaining to the innkeeper that it was not fit to eat – and a few days later he took to his bed, suffering from typhus.

Though he was lovingly cared for by his elder brother, Ferdinand, he died shortly after at the youthful age of thirty-one. One of his last wishes was that he should be buried near to Beethoven (who had died the year before), a wish that was willingly granted.

Although Schubert wrote more than a thousand songs, symphonies, operas and other forms of music, the total sum which he received for all these during his active life did not amount to more than the equivalent of five hundred and twenty-five pounds. When he died, his music manuscripts were valued at eight shillings and sixpence!

A nervous Schubert runs out of the room rather than meet Beethoven.

Well-known pieces by the Composers in this book

HANDEL

Water Music

Composed for a royal occasion on the River Thames, this well-known suite for orchestra is full of robust themes and rhythms.

Fireworks Music

Also intended for outside performance but written entirely for wind instruments. A modern arrangement for full orchestra is frequently heard.

Messiah

Surely the best known of all choral works and based on the life and influence of Jesus. Modern recordings give a truer idea of what the composer intended than do many of the live performances we might hear.

Twelve Organ Concertos

Modern recordings of these delightful pieces recapture their original lightness and clarity. At one time it was the custom to spoil the effects by using a full symphony orchestra and too much organ tone.

HAYDN

The Symphonies

Haydn wrote no less than one hundred and four symphonies and many have been given names like *The Surprise, The Clock* and *The Drum Roll*. These symphonies played a big part in helping to develop our modern orchestra.

Concerto for Trumpet and Orchestra

Many recordings of this most popular item can be heard and almost everyone will know its principal melody.

The String Quartets

Haydn was one of the first composers to show how wonderful music could be produced by only four string players. He wrote a great many quartets and perhaps the